Farm Friends Escape!

• ALL IN THE FAMILY •

A family farm is one that has been run by the same family—not a company—for many years.

Welcome Back to the Farm

he sun was shining. The morning was warm. It felt like summer. Eleven-year-old Sarah Turner giggled. Of course it felt like summer. It *was* summer! It was July. From the back seat of the car, she looked out the window. She couldn't stop smiling!

Sarah's mother was driving. "You know, Sarah," she said. "You'll be at the farm for weeks. You won't see us for a while."

"Yes," Sarah's father added. He glanced at his smiling daughter. "Try not to miss us *too* much."

"Oh, I'll miss you guys," Sarah said. "I always do. But I'm excited!" She rolled down the window. The breeze blew her ponytail. And she smiled even wider.

Sarah spent summers with her grandparents. They owned a small farm in Massachusetts. Sarah loved it there. *Wait!* Sarah thought, *I'll make a list of the things I like about the farm.* She flipped open a notebook to a blank page. She always kept a notebook nearby. She liked to organize her thoughts. Sarah wrote:

FARM LIKES
1. Animals
2. Fresh fruit

The farm had all kinds of animals. And Sarah liked each and every one.

Sarah liked the vegetables, too—but not as much as the strawberries and blueberries.

Oh! What about people? she thought. She started another list.

FARM LOVES
1. Grandma Rose and Grandpa Tom
2. Luke (when he's not joking around)

Luke was Sarah's cousin. He spent summers at the farm, too. She loved

SWEET BERRIES

Some farms let people come and pick their own fruits and vegetables. Visitors can see how food grows. They can learn about what it's like to live on a farm.

him—most of the time. They were the
same age. And, like Sarah, he was
an only child. In a way, they grew up
together during the summers with their
grandparents.

Sarah turned the notebook page.

THINGS I DON'T LIKE ABOUT
THE FARM
1. Leaving

Sarah sighed. That wasn't entirely
true. Sarah's family came from Maine.
Luke's family came from New York.
After leaving the farm, both families
always drove straight to a beach
cottage to spend a week together. It was
another Turner tradition. And Sarah
had fun being by the ocean with Luke,

MANY EARS

Most of the corn farmers grow does not end up on the dinner table. Instead, a lot is used to feed cows and other animals such as chickens. Some is turned into cooking oil. Some is used to make drinks and dessert. Some is even used to make fuel to run cars.

Chickens scratch the ground with their feet to find food.

her parents, her aunt, and uncle. But it wasn't the farm.

After driving a few hours, they turned down a dirt road. "There it is!" Sarah cried suddenly. "The farm!"

Pretty rosebushes grew next to the white house. The huge red barn stood close by. Fields and meadows spread out behind the barn. A duck pond sparkled in the sun.

Sarah's mom pulled into the driveway. Grandma Rose flung open the front door. "Tom!" she called. "They're here!"

Sarah jumped out of the car. "Grandma! I'm almost as tall as you."

When her grandfather walked over, Sarah hugged them both tightly. They smelled of grass and fresh air. They

GOT MILK?

Farmers milk their cows two times a day. On larger dairy farms, machines gently take the milk from the cows. Happy cows make more milk, so farmers take good care of their cows.

dressed alike, too, with matching jeans and boots. But Grandpa Tom was bald and serious-looking. And Grandma Rose had a long, gray braid and a cheerful grin.

Everyone hugged some more, and talked at the same time. Then another car pulled up.

"It's Luke! Yay!" cried Sarah. She ran up to the car. Luke grinned through the window. He had his summer haircut—not too long, not too short. "Open the door for me!" he shouted. He waved his hands full of candy bars.

"Okay!" Sarah tugged on the handle. It was covered in something mushy and brown. "Ugh." She jumped away. "What *is* that?"

Luke opened the door. "Peanut butter!" He laughed and handed Sarah a napkin. "Got you! Didn't I?"

A practical joke. And before he even got *out* of the car. Sarah groaned. "You are not funny, Luke!"

"Am, too."

"Are not."

"Am, too."

"No fighting," Grandpa Tom said

A-MAZE-ING!

Some farmers use hay bales to create a fun game. They place the bales in a pattern called a maze. People have to find their way to the center and back out again. Hay mazes are popular for Halloween.

sternly. "You two have to get along this summer."

Luke and Sarah stopped fussing. Grandma Rose came over. Dan, the farmhand, joined them, too.

"Hi, Dan!" said Luke and Sarah. Dan gave them big smiles. Sarah didn't expect him to say anything. Dan was quiet, but nice.

"Dan will be busy in the fields all summer," Grandpa Tom went on. "We're starting a new crop. So he won't be running the petting zoo." He looked at Sarah. Then he looked at Luke. "You will be. Together."

Sarah and Luke gasped. They were going to be in charge!

Teamwork

fter lunch Luke and Sarah said a quick goodbye to their parents. They were eager to go see the animals in the barn. The only animal they'd seen so far was the old farm dog, Duncan.

"Can we go to the barn now?" Luke asked Grandma Rose excitedly.

"Yup. Let's go!" Grandma Rose answered. "I have a lot to go over with you about the animals."

Sarah grabbed her notebook. Luke

grabbed a few peanut butter twists. And they followed Grandma Rose into the barn.

Animal stalls and pens lined the sides. The animals were quiet.

"It's their naptime," Sarah whispered.

"That's right," said Grandma Rose. "In the heat of the day, they rest."

Luke crept close to Sarah. "Mooooo!" he said loudly. She jumped. Some animals snorted and bleated. Then they quieted down.

"Luke, you know better," Grandma Rose spoke in a stern voice. But she followed it with a wink.

Sarah frowned.

Why can't Sarah relax? Luke

wondered. *Even a little bit?*

"We have some babies," Grandma Rose announced. "They are—"

"So cute!" Sarah interrupted. She and Luke rushed to the pigpen.

The tiny piglets snuffled their noses. They stayed close to their mother under the straw.

"Slow down," Grandma Rose warned. "They can't see very well. And don't pick them up. They don't like that."

"Right. Okay," Luke said, disappointed. He glanced at Sarah. She was busy scribbling notes. She kept writing as Grandma Rose went over chores and animal care.

Grandma Rose stopped by each group of animals: cows, goats, sheep, chickens, rabbits. She pointed to one rabbit. "We think Snuffles is having babies soon," she said. She talked about early feedings and late feedings. Checking hooves for rocks and twigs. Grooming and brushing.

PILE O' PIGLETS

A pig can have 12 babies, and sometimes even more! Newborn piglets nurse (drink milk from their mother) once or twice an hour.

Luke half-listened. *Sarah will take down all the information*, he thought.

Suddenly, he scooped up a fluffy hen. He examined her carefully.

"Hey, I just read about chickens," he exclaimed. "One side always has more feathers."

"Really?" Sarah looked at the hen closely. "Which side?" She held her pen ready to write.

"The outside."

Sarah laughed. *Wow! So she's got a sense of humor after all!* Luke thought. He grinned back.

Just then Grandpa Tom poked his head in. "Time for work." he announced.

"With the animals?" Luke asked.

"First comes cleaning, raking, and

painting. The petting zoo needs to be ready."

All that week and the next, Luke and Sarah worked on the petting zoo. They mended the fence around the pen. They raked and tidied. They painted the shelter. Then they filled it with hay and bedding.

Each day, they brought animals from the barn to visit the zoo. Later, they returned them to the barn. The goats nosed around, curious. The sheep stuck close together. Luke studied how the animals acted. Sarah watched them, too. The cousins would have to choose the right animals to be part of the zoo. Each animal had to have a friendly and playful personality, so they'd get along with the children.

I'd be great in a petting zoo, Luke decided. He wasn't so sure about Sarah. She was *so* serious. They were completing morning chores in the barn. And Sarah was checking her to-do list. "Organize feed bags," she read out loud. Then she called to Luke, "The quickest way to finish a job is to do it right the first time."

"Nope!" Luke answered. "The quickest way to finish a job is to move fast!" He raced across the pen, lifting four bags of chicken feed at once.

Oof! He tripped over his own feet. The bags tumbled to the ground. Feed scattered across the floor. Hens and chicks raced over to gobble it up.

LEFTOVERS

Pigs eat everything: fruits and vegetables, grains and meat. They even like to eat bugs and a little bit of dirt.

Farm Fact

OINK! OINK!

Pigs talk to one another. All those grunts, oinks, and squeals mean something.

On a farm, everyone pitches in. On many farms, kids do chores before and after school, including feeding animals and gathering eggs.

"Hey!" he called to Sarah. "You can cross 'feed the chickens' off the list."

Then he had another idea. He swept up the feed. The chickens clucked around him. "Luke is awesome," he said, sprinkling a few pellets. Bit by bit, he fed the chickens more pellets. Each time, he'd say, "Luke is awesome." After a while, when he'd say, "Luke is awesome," they'd come running.

"Pretty great trick, huh?" he asked Sarah.

Sarah wasn't paying attention. She was busy filling water bowls with the hose.

Luke sighed. He couldn't complain about Sarah too much, though. She was a hard worker. "Let's take some animals to the petting zoo," he told her.

Just as Grandma Rose had taught, they gently nudged the goats from the barn.

Suddenly, Sarah stopped. She pointed at the ground. "Candy wrappers!" She glared at Luke. "You were taking snack breaks? While I was busy working? And you littered!"

"No! I did not!" Luke sputtered.

"Who else eats peanut butter twists?" she cried.

Luke was about to answer, but the goats had trotted off. Now they were munching on Grandpa Tom's prized rose bushes. "Your fault!" shouted Luke as he and Sarah raced over.

"No! Your fault!" Sarah shouted back.

GET OFF MY BAA-CK

Goats love to climb. They even climb up on other animals!

Farm Fact

SELF-SERVICE
Goats are very smart and know how to get what they want. Scientists have taught them to solve puzzles to get their food.

Like sheep, goats graze. This means they eat grass and other types of plants.

They pulled the goats away. But
only one rose was left on each bush.
Luke groaned. They were in trouble
already. And they hadn't even opened
the petting zoo yet.

❁ ❁ ❁

Petting Zoo— Open!

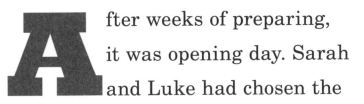

fter weeks of preparing, it was opening day. Sarah and Luke had chosen the animals for the petting zoo: two small goats named Agnes and Heidi. Daisy the cow. Two bunnies named Cuddles and Snuffles. Chickens Grace and May. And sheep Willy, Woolly, and Mo. But there was still much to do.

The cousins woke up to pouring rain

at sunrise. Luke grumbled. Sarah was too excited to care.

"The weather will clear up," Grandma Rose promised.

So Sarah and Luke pulled on raincoats and went out to the zoo. They filled feed machines. They checked soap dispensers. Visitors would have to wash their hands at the gate before they entered the zoo and as they left. This was so they and the animals wouldn't trade germs.

The cousins filled the animals' water bowls. They cleared animal droppings. They made sure the animals had fresh hay. Sarah checked each chore off her list. "Time to get the animals, then put out the sign!" she said finally.

Luke wanted to put the sign out first—*then* get the animals. Of course, Sarah disagreed. But she didn't want to argue. Not today! So they got the sign.

The big sign read: "Petting Zoo—Open" on the front. And it had a flip board in one corner. When it was lifted, the sign read "Closed." It was a good idea, Sarah thought. But the board flapped open and shut. This made it hard for them to carry the heavy sign to the entrance of the farm.

"Move faster, Luke!" Sara huffed. She didn't think she could hold on. Thankfully, Luke picked up speed.

Thud! They dropped the sign in the mud by the road. Luke righted it.

CUDDLE CORNER

Taking care of animals is a lot of work. They need food. They need water. They need a place to live that is clean, safe, and comfortable. In the winter, they need to stay warm. In the summer, they need to stay cool.

A veterinarian (an animal doctor) looks after the animals when they are sick. Animals get doctor visits when they are well, too, just like children. On a family farm, there's plenty of work for everyone.

Farm Fact

HEAT LAMP

Baby chicks get cold very easily, and need help to stay warm.

Cows can be taught to walk on a leash.

Rabbits enjoy treats in addition to their regular food.

Lambs and sheep are happiest in groups.

Baby chicks need water, food, and a warm coop.

Sarah caught her breath. "Where should we put it?"

"It's fine right here," said Luke.

"No. It needs to be in a better spot. More to the left."

"No, it doesn't."

"Yes, it does. People will see it better."

Luke ran a hand over his hair. "You know where you want it. Why did you ask me?"

"You think I'm bossy?"

"I think you came out earlier. And you decided on your own."

"I did not!"

"Yes, you did! Look!" He pointed to smudges in the mud. Footprints.

Those prints were way too big to be hers. Sarah was about to say so.

SHOW ME

At a fair, kids can show off the animals they raised themselves. The judges look to see if the animals have been well cared for. They judge how healthy the animals look. Then they pick the winners.

But then she spied someone by the trees. She couldn't make out the figure. Whoever it was had been there before. She'd thought she'd seen someone a few times, lurking near the farm. Hiding.

She had a thought. "I bet those footprints are Grandma's or Grandpa's. They're probably sneaking around, checking on us," she said.

"Hmmm," Luke said thoughtfully. "You may be right. I've felt like someone was watching us, too. They probably want to make sure we're working—and not fighting."

Luke and Sarah looked at each other and nodded. Luke moved the sign to the left. And together, they pushed the sign pole into the ground.

Next, they hurried to the barn. By now, Sarah's excitement had turned into nervousness. And it seemed she had passed on her nervous feelings to the animals. The goats wouldn't stay still. Agnes raced up the ladder to the hayloft. And when Sarah followed, Agnes raced back down. Heidi stuck her head in a bucket and couldn't get it out. Sarah pulled the bucket off. Then Snuffles and Cuddles wouldn't come out of the rabbit hutch.

PETTING ZOO HOW-TO

It's fun to pet the animals at a petting zoo. Be sure to close the gate behind you, so they don't run away. Feed them only food the farmer puts out. Other food may make them sick.

Farm Fact

CLEAN-UP TIME

Be sure to wash your hands when you leave. Sometimes animals have germs that are harmful to people.

"Maybe this will work." Luke wrinkled his nose and hopped like a bunny. "Cuddles. Snuffles. Look!" he said. He jumped around, knocking over a water bowl. He went to fill it again—then he stopped short. "Sarah! I see somebody by the trees. It's not Grandma or Grandpa."

Sarah hurried over. "Is it Dan?"

"No!" Luke pointed to a figure. "It's a kid."

"You mean a boy or girl or baby goat?" With Luke, you never knew.

"A boy. And he's watching us."

Sarah's eyes widened. "He must have left the footprints."

"And the candy wrappers," Luke added. He raced out of the petting zoo toward the kid. But the boy saw him coming. He turned and fled. Luke walked back, shrugging. "He just disappeared."

"It's just as well," Sarah said. She shook away thoughts of the suspicious boy. "Let's round up the animals. Here come Grandma and Grandpa to see if we're ready. It's time to open. We have a petting zoo to run."

✿ ✿ ✿

Escape at the Petting Zoo

he zoo had been open for more than an hour. They hadn't had one visitor. Luke felt tired already. Just getting Agnes and Heidi into the pen had been difficult. The goats hated the rain. Maybe the weather was keeping people away, too. But now the sun shone through the clouds. And still the cousins waited.

THE SCOOP ON POOP

Every day, farmers have to take away all the poop their animals make. They save it to fertilize the soil (make it richer). But first, they have to compost it. That means letting bacteria break it down into mush. Bacteria are tiny living things that can help or hurt animals and people.

The first step for turning poop into compost is to mix the poop with plant matter, such as grass clippings, leaves, or used hay. Then farmers let compost sit for a few months. Finally, they spread the compost on the soil to help the plants grow.

Farm Fact

MEADOW MUFFIN

NAME GAME
There are lots of words for poop: manure, dung, muck, cow patty, meadow muffin, road apple, horse hockey.

Clearing a place where a farm animal lives, such as a horse's stall, is called "mucking out."

Where is everybody? Luke wondered. Then he had a sudden thought. *The sign! The flip board must say the zoo is closed!*

He raced down the driveway. He was right. He flipped the sign to "Petting Zoo—Open."

Not much later, they had their first visitors: three-year-old twin boys with their parents. The boys washed their hands. They made bags of feed. They were gentle with the animals. *Easy peasy,* thought Luke.

But it was not as easy as he thought. Luke had to stop one little girl from eating goat droppings. She thought they were berries. Then he caught a little boy pulling Daisy's tail. Still, it was a lot of fun. Luke laughed as Agnes followed the children around. Those goats were always so curious, always watching people come and go.

"Luke!" Sarah was hurrying over as he filled the feed machine. "He's here!" she hissed. Immediately, Luke knew whom she meant—the suspicious boy.

"Go over to him!" Luke said. "I'll come when I'm finished."

"Me?" Sarah squeaked. Then she took a deep breath and rushed out of the pen. But a family of six was coming in at the same time. For a moment, they blocked the entrance. Sarah was stuck in the crowd. And then the boy was gone.

"It's okay," Luke told her. "That wasn't your fault. But we should tell Grandma and Grandpa. That boy is strange."

Sarah agreed.

But there were more visitors and more chores. Later, there was the afternoon feeding. Then they returned the animals to the barn and bathed some of them. By dinner, the cousins were too tired to talk. As they got ready for bed, Sarah said sleepily, "I'll write up a 'suspicious boy' list in the morning."

✿ ✿ ✿

Early the next day, Luke and Sarah brought the animals to the petting zoo. Then the cousins sat down for breakfast with their grandparents.

"We have something to tell you," Luke said. "We've seen—" He paused. "Animals!"

What a cow eats affects how much milk she makes and even how the milk tastes. If a cow eats only grass, she can make about 50 glasses of milk a day. If she also eats some corn, hay, and other foods, she can make twice as much milk.

"Of course we've seen animals!" Sarah said, annoyed. "We're on a farm. Stop joking around."

"No!" Luke gripped her arm. "Look!" He pointed to the window. Everyone stared outside.

Daisy was running past. Agnes and Heidi trotted down the driveway, right behind her.

The cousins and their grandparents jumped to their feet. The animals had escaped!

❀ ❀ ❀

On the Case

randma Rose and Grandpa Tom rushed down the driveway. Luke and Sarah raced to the pen. They hoped some animals had stayed behind. But the petting zoo was empty. No rabbits. No sheep. Not even one chicken.

"What are we going to do?" Sarah cried. Her voice rose with worry.

"Come on!" Luke grabbed her hand. They ran to their grandparents, staring down the empty road.

AN APPLE A DAY

There are more than 7,500 kinds of apples. Apples can be red, green, or yellow. Some are sweet and some are sour. Some are hard and crisp, some are soft. Some taste best right from the tree. Others taste better when you cook them.

Grandma Rose checked her watch.
"We have to make our morning
deliveries," she said to Grandpa Tom.
Each morning, they drove the farm
truck to local restaurants and grocery
stores to deliver fruits and vegetables.

"But we need to find the animals
first," said Grandpa Tom.

Luke and Sarah exchanged looks.
Their grandparents had a business to run.
Sarah felt she and Luke could handle it
on their own. "You can go," she told them.
"We can take care of the animals."

"Definitely!" Luke agreed.

Grandpa shook his head no. He
didn't say anything. Maybe he thought
they had left the zoo's gate open.

But Luke was already steering

them toward the truck. "We know the animals, Grandpa. The animals know us. We can do it!"

"Tom." Grandma Rose touched his arm. "Today is the first day we deliver to that big supermarket. The truck is already loaded. We really shouldn't be late." She smiled at the cousins. "I trust Luke and Sarah."

After more discussion, Grandpa Tom agreed. Grandma Rose would make calls while he drove. She'd let neighbors know to look out for the animals. "And Dan is already on his way here," she said. "He will help."

"We'll make our deliveries quickly," Grandpa said.

Seconds later, the truck roared off.

Sarah's heart raced. Their grandparents were gone. All of a sudden, she didn't feel so sure of things. "Now what?" she asked.

"We act fast!" said Luke. "Let's search around the petting zoo again."

The still-empty pen seemed strange, Sarah thought. And a little spooky. Was that Cuddles in the corner? She rushed closer. No—it wasn't the rabbit. It was only leaves.

"How did they escape?" Luke was puzzled. "We need to look for clues. Did you stack the feed buckets last night?" Luke asked.

"Yes."

"Well, look. They're scattered around now."

Self-Serve

TOM
STRING
SWEE

ROADSIDE ATTRACTION
Some farmers sell their extra fruits and vegetables in a farm stand. That's a little store on the side of the road. Everything in the farm stand is super fresh.

STRAWBERRIES

Sweet and delicious, these berries grow low to the ground. They are ripe in the spring.

WATERMELONS

This summer favorite grows on a vine. The heavy fruit rests on the ground.

EGGPLANTS

Sun and warm weather help this vegetable grow.

TOMATOES

They were first grown in South America. Now people all over the world love them.

"*Hmmm.* And those crates are in different spots, too." Sarah pointed out two crates, overturned by the gate. "Looks like somebody snuck in and messed around. Do you think it's that boy?"

She gazed toward the trees. She almost expected the boy to be there, lurking as before. Then she noticed something.

"Hey!" she exclaimed. "Footprints!" In the mud, between the zoo and trees, were more prints. These were clear and easy to see.

"Sneaker prints!" said Luke.

It had to be that kid!

CHAPTER 6

Rounding Up the Runaways

**H**ow could that boy do *this?* Luke wondered. He understood about pranks and practical jokes. He figured the boy might think this would be funny. But it put the animals in danger. He and Sarah had to find them.

"Where would they go?" Luke asked.

Sarah thought out loud. "The sheep and goats will stay in groups. That should make it easier."

"Okay, then." Luke tapped his foot impatiently. "Let's get going. It's better if we split up."

They divided responsibilities. Luke headed to the small wooded area. He'd stay near the farm, in case animals came back. This had to work out!

✿ ✿ ✿

Sarah hopped on a bike to search the neighborhood. *Sheep,* she thought. *Where would they go? They couldn't have gone too far. What was close by?*

Last summer she and Luke had spent days searching a field for four-leaf clover. That field was just down the road. She knew sheep loved clover. The field would be perfect for grazing. Sarah pedaled away.

In no time, the field came into view. *Yes!* Sarah pumped her fist. Three fluffy shapes were in the far corner—Willy, Woolly, and Mo. They bent their heads and grazed.

"Yes!" Sarah shouted. In the quiet of the morning, her cry rang out loudly. The sheep twitched, startled. Sheep have excellent hearing, Sarah knew. She shouldn't scare them. They might take off again.

Sarah did not move. After a few moments, the sheep went back to grazing. She inched forward quietly. Bit by bit, she drew closer. Finally, she

● LIVING LAWNMOWERS ●

Sheep like to graze (feed on) tasty grasses. They will move from area to area as they eat. Sheep like to stay together in groups to graze. When one sheep heads to a new area, the others follow.

Wide-set eyes allow sheep to see things behind them without turning their heads.

Farm Fact

SNACK TIME!

In addition to grass, sheep munch on other plants in the pasture. Favorites include clover and sunflowers.

stood next to them. She scratched their
ears and smiled.

But how could she bring them back
to the farm? They wouldn't want to go.
Not with all this clover to eat!

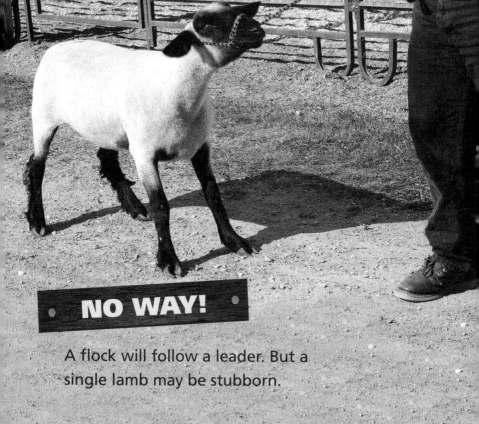

NO WAY!

A flock will follow a leader. But a
single lamb may be stubborn.

She tried pushing and prodding the sheep. First, Willy, then Woolly, then Mo. *Just one*, she thought. If one got moving, the other two would follow. But Sarah was out of luck. Not one sheep budged.

What else could she do? Who could help? She had an idea: *Duncan! He is a herding dog, after all.*

In a flash, Sarah rode home. She brought Duncan back. Excited to be outside, he ran next to the bike. *He's almost like a puppy again,* Sarah thought.

Then Duncan saw the sheep. "Go on, boy," Sarah said. "Let's take them home."

Immediately, Duncan went into action. He nosed the sheep away from the field. Then he ran ahead to show them the way. And he doubled back to prod them. Again and again, he urged them forward. Sarah rode next to them so they wouldn't veer off path. It took a while. But Sarah and Duncan herded the sheep right back into the petting zoo.

In the distance, Sarah saw Luke. He was searching around the trees. "I got the sheep!" she called.

"Good! Try for the goats," he shouted back.

"If you were a goat, where would you go?" she asked Duncan. The dog cocked his head, as if he were thinking. "You'd like to jump and climb, so . . ." Sarah suddenly snapped her fingers.

"What about a playground?"

She and Luke

had played at the elementary school playground many times. The goats might have gone in that direction. The school was the opposite way from the clover field. She took a deep breath. It would be a long bike ride.

Beep! Beep! Dan pulled into the driveway in his pickup truck just then. Sarah ran over, and explained everything.

"Hop in!" said Dan.

Sarah and Duncan jumped into the truck. Dan drove fast. Sarah looked all around, in case the goats were on the road. Minutes later, they reached the school. Dan swung around the building, and parked at the edge of the playground.

"They're here!" Sarah cried.

Two towers stood at either end of a giant climbing structure. A bridge connected them. *Maaa. Maaa.* Agnes was trotting across the bridge. *Clop, clop.* Sarah almost laughed. Maybe there was a troll underneath, like in "The Three Billy Goats Gruff."

Heidi stepped onto the bottom of a seesaw. She started up the board. As she skipped past the middle, the other side went down. And she skipped even faster. At the end, she turned around to do it all over again.

Sarah, Dan, and Duncan hopped out of the truck. "Duncan!" Sarah called. "Herding time!"

But Duncan just lay in the shade,

• BORDER PATROL •

Border collies control sheep using a special look called "the eye." They lower their head and stare at the sheep to make them move.

Farm Fact

ALL ACTION

Border collies need lots of things to do. They have tons of energy and like to play.

For some breeds (types) of dogs, herding is a natural skill. In a family home, a herder may nudge a family member toward the dog food dish.

panting. The poor old dog was hot and tired. He'd be no help now. Sarah watched Agnes. Maybe she and Dan could catch Agnes first. The goat was skidding down a slide. Sarah moved closer. Dan moved closer. But Agnes scampered away quickly. She darted around the swings. She leaped over benches. She moved so fast, they didn't have a chance to grab her.

Maybe Heidi, Sarah thought.

But Heidi was scooting up the climbing mountain now. When Sarah reached for her, she jumped off and raced away.

"We'll never get them!" Sarah groaned.

"I may have something we can use

to pen them in," Dan said quietly. "I think I have some fencing." He reached under a tarp in the back of the truck. Then he took out two mesh rolls. He and Sarah unrolled them, then waited. Minutes later, both goats stopped under the bridge to chew on a pile of twigs.

Sarah cried, "Now!"

Working at top speed, she and Dan set up the fences around the towers. The goats were trapped.

"Oh, Agnes," Sarah said, reaching in to hug her close. "You silly thing." She led Agnes onto the truck, and Dan got Heidi.

"Duncan!" Sarah called. "Home!"

The dog raced over. "*Now* he's running." Sarah laughed.

Dan drove to the farm, and they took the goats into the petting zoo. The sheep were in the shelter, and now Agnes and Heidi were, too. The animals all grew quiet, eating and resting after their big adventure.

Dan headed off to continue the search. Sarah sighed and looked around. She didn't see Luke anywhere.

"*Woof!*" Duncan herded Sarah into the house. "I know, I know," she said. "You want to eat, too!"

She'd feed Duncan, then go find Luke. Sarah crossed her fingers for luck. She only hoped Luke and the other animals were okay.

Follow the Footprints

Luke, meanwhile, had found two sets of animal prints in the mud. Following them, he stepped into the wooded area behind the barn. He bent to examine the prints. One set looked like a cow's hooves. *Daisy,* he thought. The other set looked like arrows. Chicken prints—Grace and May.

Daisy first, Luke decided. He tracked the hoofprints around the trees. When

HOOVES

Many farm animals walk on hooves. A hoof is a hard covering at the end of a foot. Hooves are made of the same stuff as your fingernails.

HORSE

TWO-PART HOOVES

Some animal hooves have two parts. Pigs, goats, sheep, and cows have two-part hooves.

GOAT

WEBBED FEET

Ducks and geese have extra skin between their toes, called webbing. Webbed feet act like paddles. They make ducks and geese good swimmers.

GOOSE

PADDED FEET

Dogs, cats, and rabbits all have soft pads on their feet. The pads help them run fast and land softly.

CAT

the dirt and tracks ended, Luke looked around. He was at the edge of a meadow. And Daisy was happily munching on grass. She looked up and saw him. Then she went back to grazing.

"Daisy, Daisy," Luke said softly. He just wanted to grab onto her quickly. But he held himself back. He didn't want to spook her.

"How are you doing, Daisy?" Luke kept talking in a soothing voice. Slowly, he edged closer. Finally, he took hold of her collar. *Got you!* he thought. Still moving slowly, he led her home.

Back at the pen, Luke peered into the shelter. The goats and sheep were inside. Immediately, Luke felt better. He didn't see Sarah. But that was okay.

They were making progress. There were just the chickens and rabbits left. And he had an idea where the chickens had gone.

He passed a feed bucket, and stopped. Why hadn't he thought of this earlier? They could use food to get the animals home! He grabbed the bucket. He hurried back to follow the chicken prints.

Luke followed the trail for a few feet. But then the prints stopped. They didn't go left or right. They just disappeared. How could that be?

"Okay," he said out loud. "Chickens can't just disappear."

Why hadn't he listened more closely when Grandma Rose talked about animal behavior? Then he remembered

one important fact. Chickens can fly!
At least a bit. So he gazed up into a
tree close by. There, on a low branch,
sat Grace and May. *Cluck! Cluck!* They
seemed happy. And in no hurry to leave.

"Luke is awesome," Luke called
softly. He tossed some feed under the
branch. Still clucking, they hopped
right off.

"Luke is awesome!" Luke repeated,
starting back to the farm. He left a trail
of feed. The chickens followed behind,
pecking at the food. Finally they
reached the pen. "Whew!" Luke sighed.
He had just run out of feed.

"Luke!" Sarah called, hurrying into
the pen. "I was just feeding Duncan in
the house." Then she grinned. "You got

HIGH BAR

Some chickens have an outside yard with a little house called a chicken coop. They like to sleep inside the coop. The farmer puts pieces of wood called roosting bars around the coop for the chickens to sleep on.

Farm Fact

COZY

Mother chickens, called hens, have nesting boxes inside the coop. This is where they lay their eggs.

Chickens feel safer
when they are
sleeping up high.

Daisy and the chickens!" She held up her hand for a high five. "Awesome!"

Luke raised his hand, too. But at the word "awesome," the chickens rose in the air. They squawked and flapped their wings, looking for food. Luke and Sarah slapped away the feathers.

"Forget it, Sarah," said Luke, laughing. Then he turned serious. "Now let's find those rabbits."

A Double Surprise

arah grabbed carrots for rabbit bait. "Let's search by the duck pond, Luke," she said.

Together, they walked toward a bunch of trees. Just a few steps in, they found Cuddles snuggled on the ground by a tree trunk. The poor rabbit was shivering. His ears were flat. He was scared. Sarah crouched closer. "Cuddles," she whispered. "We're here. It's okay." She held out a carrot.

BUNNY BABIES

Rabbits are born with their eyes closed and without fur. They have some fur by the time they are 7 days old. Their eyes open after about 10 or 11 days.

Farm Fact

LEGGING IT

Rabbits have really strong back legs. This helps them run fast. They can also kick with their back legs to protect themselves.

These bunnies will stay in the nest for about a month. Then they can hop off on their own.

He sniffed it, then nibbled, and relaxed as Sarah petted him.

"Okay, now where's Snuffles?" Luke asked. Cuddles began to hop down a path. "Maybe he knows!" Sarah said.

The cousins started along the trail behind him. They edged around a bend. Then they stopped short. Luke gasped.

"It's you!" Sarah exclaimed.

The suspicious boy was standing in the middle of the path. Up close, Sarah could see he had freckles and dark brown eyes. The boy faced them, crossing his arms. *It's like he's guarding something,* Sarah thought. *He won't let us pass.*

Behind the boy, a small furry creature dug under leaves. "It's Snuffles! He's got Snuffles!" Sarah cried.

Luke quickly scooped up Cuddles and held him tight.

"I have a name," the boy said. "It's Pete."

"Okay, Pete," said Luke angrily. "We want our rabbit back!"

"No!" Pete replied.

Sarah's heart sank. What would they do now? Call their grandparents? Dan? The police?

"You can't move her," Pete went on. "I think she's about to have babies."

"Our grandma already *told* us Snuffles was having babies," Luke snickered. "But what makes *you* the rabbit expert? How do you know it's about to happen *now*?"

Pete blushed. "Well, I've always

PETS ON A FARM

BARN BUDDY

Cats are welcome on a farm. They keep mice away from the other animals' food.

LITTLE PIGGIES

Guinea pigs like to live with other guinea pigs. When they are happy, they purr, just like a cat.

HEE-HAW

Donkeys are strong and smart. They like to live in groups. But if there are no other donkeys around, they will make friends with goats.

wanted a pet rabbit. So I've done a ton of reading." He looked down at Snuffles. "She's trying to build a nest. See?"

Snuffles was busy collecting grass and twigs. She even pulled out some of her fur, using her teeth. She added the fur to the pile. Then she burrowed under it all.

"Well, maybe you're right," Sarah said to Pete. "But what should we do?"

"We could help," Pete said quietly. "Do you have a nest box?"

"Yes!" said Sarah. "We could use it to carry her back to the farm."

"Good idea," Luke agreed. "Snuffles and her babies will be safer there."

Sarah raced to the barn and back, holding the box. Then she and Luke carefully lifted Snuffles with the grass, and twigs, and fur into the nest box. Luke carried the box. Sarah carried Cuddles.

She told Luke when to watch out for rocks on the path. And Pete trailed behind.

Back at the barn, the cousins placed the box in the rabbit hutch. The babies came in minutes. Sarah and Luke glimpsed the babies. There were five altogether. They were tiny, without any fur. Snuffles covered them with her own fur, like a blanket.

"We got her back just in time," Sarah whispered.

"Good job, Snuffles," Luke said softly.

All at once, Sarah realized Pete hadn't come into the barn. He was waiting outside.

"Hey, thanks, for your help," Luke told him as they stepped through the doors. "But we have to ask you something. Why have you been watching us?"

Pete looked down, embarrassed.

"Well, I love all animals. Not just rabbits. That's why I've been hanging around."

"You should have just come to the petting zoo!" Sarah exclaimed.

"That's the crazy thing." Pete spoke in a low voice. "I love animals. But I'm scared of them. I don't want to get too close." He looked at the cousins nervously. "I know it's lame. But watching you take care of the animals— it's the closest I've come to petting one."

Sarah and Luke burst out laughing.

"Go ahead and laugh," Pete said miserably. "I know it's ridiculous."

"No, that's not it." Sarah said. "I'm

afraid of lots of things. But we thought you were up to something. You know, something suspicious."

"So *you* didn't let the animals out?" Luke asked.

Pete shook his head. "I'd never do that."

"Well—that takes care of one mystery," Sarah said.

"Yeah, and it leaves a bigger one," Luke added.

How did the animals escape?

❀ ❀ ❀

CHAPTER 9

Mystery Solved

After Pete went home, the animals came out of the petting zoo shelter. They all seemed rested. Finally able to relax, too, Luke and Sarah sat in a corner watching them.

"Look at Agnes!" Luke whispered curiously. The cousins watched in amazement.

The small goat pushed a crate to a feeding machine. Then she stood on the crate to reach a knob on the machine.

She took the knob in her mouth. Then she turned it. Feed poured out of the chute. The other animals trotted over.

The cousins looked at each other, amazed. They'd had the same thought. *Could Agnes have unlocked the gate?*

Luke couldn't believe it. "Let's test it out."

He carried the crate to the gate. Right away, Agnes skipped over. She climbed on top and stretched her neck toward the lock. She slid the bolt, using her mouth. The gate swung open.

"Maaa! Maaa!" she called to the other animals. They filed behind her, and began to head out.

"Whoa! Wait!" Sarah pushed them back inside. Luke bolted the lock again.

"Well, that solves the mystery," he said. "And just in time." Grandma Rose and Grandpa Tom were driving up. And so was Dan.

"Everyone's back!" said Grandma Rose, smiling.

Grandpa Tom checked the animals carefully. "Nice work," he finally said.

The cousins told them everything— from rounding up the animals, to

RUNNING AROUND

Goats are social. They hang out in groups and are friendly with people. They are smart, too. And they really like to climb.

Farm Fact

UP IN A TREE

In Morocco, goats hang out in trees! They like to eat the tasty nuts and leaves of argan trees.

Groups of goats, called herds, have leaders and followers. They may bite and butt heads to work out which one will be leader.

meeting Pete, to Snuffles having babies, to Agnes opening the gate lock.

"How did you manage to do all this?" Grandpa asked, ruffling Luke's hair and tugging on Sarah's ponytail. The cousins beamed.

"Well, we've learned a lot these past few weeks," said Sarah.

"And today, we learned one more important thing," Luke added. Sarah groaned. It sounded like the lead up to a bad joke.

"To keep goats in the pen," Luke continued, "we need to move the lock to the *outside* of the gate!"

"And get that crate out of here, too!" said Sarah.

Summer's End

The weeks passed quickly. Pete came to the farm every day. It turned out he and his parents had recently moved in down the road. It had been hard leaving his friends, Pete explained. And his older brother hadn't even been around. He'd been traveling with friends.

"Pete's like a little lost lamb," Sarah had told Luke. "We need to make him part of the farm."

So bit by bit, the cousins worked

with Pete. And bit by bit, Pete grew relaxed with the farm animals. He helped feed them. He helped groom them. By the end of the summer, he was doing chores on his own.

"See?" Luke joked. "That was our plan all along. To have you do all the work!"

Soon the nights grew cooler, the days shorter. Summer was ending. In no time, it was Luke and Sarah's last day on the farm. Their grandparents prepared a farewell picnic lunch. Grandma Rose spread a blanket by the duck pond. Dan helped Grandpa Tom put out fresh fruits and vegetables. Pete and his parents came, bringing sandwiches and peanut butter twists.

After lunch, Luke stood up. "And now,"

he said in a deep announcer voice, "We have a special presentation." He pulled Sarah to her feet. They turned to Pete. "We talked to our grandparents. And our grandparents talked to your parents. And we all decided you should have—"

"An end-of-summer gift." Sarah announced. She lifted two baby bunnies from a carrying case.

"I thought that was another picnic basket!" Pete exclaimed. He grinned from ear to ear. "You mean these bunnies . . . Crackers! Crumbles! They're mine?"

"That's right, honey," Pete's mom said, smiling.

"We know you'll take good care of them," Grandpa Tom added.

"You'd better!" put in Luke. "We'll be

FARM BABIES

Baby animals are busy. Sometimes they hang out together. At other times they cuddle with mom. And when they're ready, they take their first step, hop, or flight.

Puppies love to run, jump, and play. Then it's time for a long nap!

Baby geese, called goslings, practice using their wings before their feathers grow in.

Baby chicks can't fly until their wing feathers grow in. But they can jump!

Calves (baby cows) have knobby knees and a wobbly walk.

Lambs talk to one another in bleats that sound like *baa* and *meh*.

A bed of straw in a quiet spot makes a perfect nest for a female barn cat and her kittens.

back to check on them, you know."

"And that's why it's not so hard saying goodbye," said Sarah. "We'll all be together next summer."

Grandma Rose nodded. "There will be lots to do. We've decided to open a farm stand near the petting zoo."

"You'll be in charge of that, too," Grandpa Tom said. "So get ready to work twice as hard."

❁ ❁ ❁

Luke and Sarah's parents came that afternoon. There were hugs, kisses, and some tears as they said goodbye to their grandparents. Then the cousins were on their way to vacation at the ocean cottage.

As soon as they arrived, it was
time for the beach. Sarah got ready
quickly. If they hurried, they could see
the sunset. She waited impatiently for
Luke. "What's taking so long?" she
asked.

"I'm checking my list," Luke said.
"Towels . . . camera . . . peanut butter
twists . . ." The list went on and on.

"Why, Luke," Sarah teased. "You
sound just like me. You have everything
except the kitchen sink. Here!" She
pretended to pull up the sink.

Luke laughed. "And you're joking
around like me!" He grinned. "Only
you're not as funny."

Just then a neighbor came to the
door. He looked upset. "Have you seen a

black-and-white cat?" he asked. "Ours ran away."

Luke and Sarah looked at each other. The beach could wait. They were ready to help!

✿ ✿ ✿

FUN IN THE SUN

When chores are done, it's time
to have some fun!

CREDITS AND ACKNOWLEDGMENTS

Writer Gail Herman
Illustrator Bryan Langdo
Produced by Scout Books & Media Inc
President and Project Director Susan Knopf
Editor Sonia Black
Managing Editor Brittany Gialanella
Copyeditor Beth Adelman
Editorial Intern Margaret A. Shaffer
Proofreader Michael Centore
Designer Annemarie Redmond

Thanks to the Time Inc. Books team: Margot Schupf, Anja Schmidt, Beth Sutinis, Deirdre Langeland, Georgia Morrissey, Megan Pearlman, Melodie George, and Sue Chodakiewicz.

Special thanks to the Discovery and Animal Planet creative and licensing teams: Denny Chen, Carolann Dunn, Elizabeta Ealy, Robert Marick, Doris Miller, and Janet Tsuei.